Munsch at Play

Act 2

Eight More Stage Adaptations

Plays by Irene N. Watts

Original Stories by Robert Munsch

Illustrated by Michael Martchenko

We acknowledge the support of the Canada Council for the Arts, the Ontario Arts Council, and the Government
of Canada through the Canada Book Fund (CBF) for our publishing activities.

 ONTARIO ARTS COUNCIL
CONSEIL DES ARTS DE L'ONTARIO

Cataloging in Publication

Watts, Irene N., 1931-
     Munsch at play act 2 : eight more stage adaptations : plays / by Irene N. Watts ; original stories
by Robert Munsch ; illustrated by Michael Martchenko.

ISBN 978-1-55451-358-1

     1. Munsch, Robert N., 1945- —Adaptations. I. Munsch, Robert N., 1945- II. Martchenko, Michael III. Title.

PS8595.A873M87 2011   jC812'.54   C2011-900881-5

Distributed in Canada by:

Firefly Books Ltd.
66 Leek Crescent
Richmond Hill, ON
L4B 1H1

Published in the U.S.A. by:

Annick Press (U.S.) Ltd.
Distributed in the U.S.A. by:
Firefly Books (U.S.) Inc.
P.O. Box 1338
Ellicott Station
Buffalo, NY 14205

Printed in China.

Visit us at: www.annickpress.com

Visit Robert Munsch at: www.robertmunsch.com

Visit Irene Watts at: www.irenenwatts.com

For Meghan, Morgan, and Hannah
—I.N.W.

Contents

★ Preface ★

How many ways are there to tell a story? How many ways can you dramatize Robert Munsch's well-loved tales? Like the first volume of *Munsch at Play*, this second volume offers a starting point for you and your cast's creativity. The ideas in *Act 2* are suggestions for you to build on and not intended to be cast in stone! As one reader wrote:

My children just love the idea of dramatizing—the enjoyment is not diminished by lack of spectators.

But I assume that for most groups the plays will be shared with an audience in class or elsewhere. There are no restrictions on where the plays can be presented: in the classroom, the library or gymnasium, or any suitable space, both indoors or outdoors. Groups have performed in community and senior centers, for other schools, at day camps, in public libraries, and at festivals.

The audience may surround the actors completely or sit in a horseshoe (U shape), observing the action from three sides, or in a long hallway watching from both sides of an alley. Spectators will, I hope, become participants too!

Actors may be in full sight of their audience at all times, changing character and costume without leaving the stage. Their exits and entrances can consist of a simple turn upstage or getting up

from their places on stage in full view of the audience to participate in the action. At other times, the conventional entrance and exit to and from the stage are used.

- For those new to drama, the following approach may provide a useful beginning: The story is read aloud by the teacher/leader and discussed as a class.
- In groups, the story is read again, talked through, cast, and improvised by students, who at first use their own words.
- Each group then presents its improvisation, and a discussion takes place about any new ideas that emerged in presentation. Was double or even triple casting used? Was the story shared in the telling so that everyone in the group took part?
- What sound effects were used? What kind of space was chosen? Did students find and use props, use mime, or a combination of both? Each group *hopefully* should open up a new way of looking, listening, and telling.
- Did groups interpret the story in an unusual way? In *From Far Away*, one group used tableaux to illustrate the idea of war.
- The artist's interpretation gives wonderful hints regarding character, costume, and set design! Why not encourage students to volunteer to be in charge of technical aspects, such as artwork, props to make or find, and costumes?
- *Optional:* A useful rehearsal strategy is to take the group on a

field trip to a fire station, police station, farm, or subway. If this is not a realistic option, invite a speaker to class to discuss his or her experiences, such as a recent resident to Canada (*From Far Away*) or someone in the moving business (*David's Father*). For each of the plays, a relevant talk or a field trip brings new insight to story research.

Rehearsal Reminders:

- Actors are responsible for and must check their own props.
- Actors must listen to the story no matter how familiar they are with it—one actor fidgeting or not listening will distract the audience. Let students demonstrate this to the class for maximum impact! In a row of attentive actors, when one turns his head, the audience is distracted.
- Most important is freshness. The actor tells his part of the story as if he was saying unrehearsed words. Each time the story is presented it needs to be discovered anew.
- A technical rehearsal for exits, entrances, costumes, and props is vital and may highlight a problem spot where the actors need more or less time. For casts that have decided to use mime, and as a fun warm-up activity, *What Am I Doing?* challenges students in several ways: It may be done solo, in twos, threes, or in groups. A few minutes are allowed to decide on the action—going upstairs, driving a car or truck,

climbing a mountain, eating dinner, getting ready for a party, or becoming lost! When the mime is complete, the performer asks, "What am I doing?" Three guesses are allowed before the challenger must repeat the actions using words.

Running Time:

Each play takes about 10 minutes to perform, but depending on the size of cast, space, and amount of audience participation, extra time may be needed.

Enjoy!

Irene N. Watts

The Fire Station

CAST

- Narrators 1 and 2
- Michael
- Sheila
- Large Firefighter
- Firefighters (four to eight)
- Fire Chief
- Fire (created by Props Assistants and Cast not playing Firefighters)
- Michael's Mother
- Sheila's Father
- Police Officers (two)
- Prisoner
- Props Assistants (one for each Narrator)

STAGING

The play may be performed onstage or in any open space. ACTORS sit around a half-square or horseshoe (U shape), facing the audience. A center aisle between the playing space and the seated audience is helpful for SHEILA and MICHAEL's walks.

ACTORS may create an entrance or exit in different ways:

Audiences will accept a simple turn upstage. ACTORS may put on a costume piece in view of the audience and enter the playing area from their places onstage, returning to their seats when finished, or they may enter or exit from offstage—behind screens or from wings (on a conventional stage) or whatever masking device is used.

ACTORS seated in view of the audience sit as still as possible, with their attention on the NARRATORS and the action taking place in front of them.

At the start of the play, the NARRATORS are seated close to the audience at stage right or left across from each other. A PROPS ASSISTANT is seated on the floor beside each NARRATOR, or on a small bench, which can serve to hold props and to help create the large fire truck.

The NARRATORS may be seated on any raised level—a stool, chair, cube, or riser. NARRATORS and their ASSISTANTS take their places onstage before the audience comes in. ACTORS file in from behind the audience, up the center aisle, to go to their places. MICHAEL and SHEILA are at the back of the audience area waiting for the NARRATORS to begin the story.

SET DESIGN

- two sets of risers—preset upstage right
- one or two stepladders—preset upstage left
- a hat/coat stand for the FIREFIGHTERS' helmets
- A screen, an old-fashioned clothes horse, or rolling blackboard, to which the location names are pinned or murals of a fire station or police station are attached. These are also used to mask stage entrances and exits from upstage.
- seats for NARRATORS at downstage right and left

PROPS AND COSTUMES

Actors are responsible for their own props and must do a final check both onstage and offstage before the start of the play. It is also important to do a run-through only for exits, entrances, and props and costumes toward the end of the rehearsal period.

- a piece of doweling for each PROPS ASSISTANT
- two oversized tie-dyed T-shirts in fire colors for MICHAEL and SHEILA
- fire helmets for FIREFIGHTERS (with a special badge for the FIRE CHIEF)
- police hats (two)
- rubber boots
- hoses made from lengths of cloth, paper towel rolls, or papier-mâché
- bubble mixture
- toy fire trucks of different sizes (optional) that ACTORS hold up on cue
- notebooks and pens or pencils for the POLICE OFFICERS
- a cutout representing a large fire truck. Handgrips inside help CAST to hold it upright.
- fire streamers for PROPS ASSISTANTS and CAST who are not FIREFIGHTERS
- Optional: Instead of murals, a FIRE STATION sign and a POLICE STATION sign could be held up by either a NARRATOR or a PROPS ASSISTANT.

NARRATOR 1:	This story is called *The Fire Station*.
	(MICHAEL and SHEILA walk up the center aisle from back of the audience.)
NARRATOR 1:	Michael and Sheila were walking down the street. When they passed the fire station, Sheila said:
SHEILA:	Michael! Let's go ride a fire truck.
MICHAEL:	Well, I think maybe I should ask my mother, and I think maybe …
SHEILA:	I think we should go in.
NARRATOR 1:	Said Sheila, then she grabbed Michael's hand and pulled him up to the door of the fire station, Sheila knocked.
CAST:	Blam-Blam-Blam-Blam-Blam.
	(Sound made by voices, fists on floor, and dowels used by the PROPS ASSISTANTS. A LARGE FIREFIGHTER in a peaked hat appears from the upcenter "door.")
NARRATOR 1:	A large firefighter came out and asked:
LARGE FIREFIGHTER:	What can I do for you?
MICHAEL:	Well, maybe you could show us a fire truck and hoses and rubber boots and ladders and all sorts of stuff like that.
LARGE FIREFIGHTER:	Certainly.

NARRATOR 1:   Said the firefighter.

SHEILA: And maybe you will let us drive a fire
                     truck?

NARRATOR 1:   Said Sheila.

LARGE FIREFIGHTER: Certainly not.

NARRATOR 1:   Said the firefighter.

NARRATOR 2:   They went in and looked at ladders and
                     hoses and big rubber boots. Then they
                     looked at little fire trucks and big fire
                     trucks. *(Cue for seated CAST to stand and
                     hold up toy trucks and sit again on the next
                     line.)*

NARRATOR 2:   And enormous fire trucks. *(A large cutout
                     of a fire truck is held up by the PROPS
                     ASSISTANTS, and ACTORS crouch upstage
                     of this. Alternatively, the cast may create
                     the truck with risers, ladders, and the
                     bench as the back seat for MICHAEL and
                     SHEILA—or the truck may be totally
                     mimed.)*

NARRATOR 2:   When they were done, Michael said:

MICHAEL: Let's go.

SHEILA: Right, let's go into the enormous truck.

NARRATOR 2:   Said Sheila.

NARRATOR 1:	While they were in the truck, the fire alarm went off:
CAST:	Clang-Clang-Clang-Clang-Clang.
MICHAEL:	Oh no!
NARRATOR 1:	Said Michael.
SHEILA:	Oh yes!
NARRATOR 1:	Said Sheila. Then she grabbed Michael and pulled him into the back seat.
NARRATOR 2:	Firefighters came running from all over. They slid down poles *(mimed)* and ran down stairs *(all grab boots and helmets)*, then they jumped onto the truck and drove off. The firefighters didn't look in the back seat AND …
CAST:	Michael and Sheila were in the back seat.
NARRATOR 2:	They came to an enormous fire. Lots of yucky-colored smoke got all over everything
	(CAST/PROPS ASSISTANTS move around the performance area waving fire streamers or ribbons. ASSISTANTS throw tie-dyed T-shirts over MICHAEL and SHEILA.)
NARRATOR 2:	The fire colored Michael yellow, green, and blue. It colored Sheila purple, green, and yellow.

(FIREFIGHTERS use hoses on the fire.)

NARRATOR 2:   When the fire chief saw them he said:

FIRE CHIEF: What are you doing here?

NARRATOR 2:   Sheila said:

SHEILA: We came in the fire truck. We thought
                   maybe it was a taxi. We thought, maybe …
                   it was an elevator.

MICHAEL: We thought, maybe …

FIRE CHIEF: I think, MAYBE, I'd better take you home.

NARRATOR 2:   Said the fire chief.

                   *(The fire truck is dismantled and the
                   firefighters return to their places.)*

NARRATOR 2:   The fire chief put Michael and Sheila in his
                   car and drove them away.

                   *(The FIRE CHIEF, MICHAEL, and SHEILA sit
                   right or left, facing upstage. A short freeze
                   while any signs, fire props, boots, and hel-
                   mets are removed. MICHAEL and SHEILA
                   rise and face front, then they walk around
                   the stage.)*

NARRATOR 1:   When Michael got home, he knocked on
                   the door. His mother opened it and said:

MOTHER: You messy boy! You can't come in and play
                   with Michael! You're too dirty.

NARRATOR 1:	She slammed the door right in Michael's face. *(MOTHER exits.)*
MICHAEL:	My own mother, she didn't even know me.
NARRATOR 1:	Said Michael and knocked on the door again. His mother opened the door and said:
MOTHER:	You dirty boy! You can't come in and play with Michael. You're too dirty. You're absolutely filthy. You're a total mess. You're … Oh my! Oh no! … YOU'RE MICHAEL! *(MOTHER grabs MICHAEL and drags him inside. SHEILA starts to walk away, then circles the stage the moment MOTHER and MICHAEL exit.)*
NARRATOR 1:	Michael went inside and lived in the bath-tub for three whole days:
CAST:	Day one … *(A T-shirt is thrown up in the air offstage so it is visible to the audience, and bubbles from preset bubbles offstage fill the air throughout the next sequence.)*
CAST:	Day two … Day three …
NARRATOR 1:	Until he got clean. *(SHEILA reaches home. MICHAEL enters and sits with the CAST.)*

NARRATOR 2:	When Sheila came home, she knocked on the door. Her father opened it and saw an incredibly messy girl. He said:
FATHER:	You can't come in to play with Sheila. You're too dirty. *(Exits)*
NARRATOR 2:	He slammed the door right in her face.
SHEILA:	OW, my own father and he didn't even know me.
NARRATOR 2:	Said Sheila, and she kicked and pounded on the door as loudly as she could. Her father opened the door and said:
FATHER:	Now stop that racket, you dirty girl. You can't come in to play with Sheila. You're too dirty. You're absolutely filthy. You're a total mess! You're … Oh my! … Oh no! … YOU'RE SHEILA!
SHEILA:	Right, I went to a fire in the back of a fire truck and I got all smoky AND I WASN'T EVEN SCARED.
NARRATOR 2:	Said Sheila and went inside and lived in the bathtub for FIVE DAYS! *(The same procedure, with T-shirt and bubbles, as for MICHAEL)*
CAST:	Day one … Day two … Day three … Day four … Day five …
NARRATOR 2:	Until she got clean.

(SHEILA enters and is joined by MICHAEL.)

NARRATOR 1:   Then Michael took Sheila on a walk past the police station.

(A sign says POLICE STATION. The PROPS ASSISTANTS turn the ladder sideways, each holds one end. Two POLICE OFFICERS take the PRISONER and place him behind bars. They then move downstage, observing the audience and writing comments in their notebooks.)

NARRATOR 1:   Michael told her:

MICHAEL: If you ever take me in another fire truck, I am going to ask the police to put you in … JAIL!

SHEILA: JAIL?

NARRRATOR 2:   Yelled Sheila.

SHEILA: Let's go look at the jail! What a great idea!

MICHAEL: Oh no!

NARRATOR 2:   Yelled Michael, but Sheila grabbed his hand and pulled him into the police station.

(Freeze. The ladder is removed. MOTHER and FATHER join CAST onstage. All bow.)

I Have to Go!

CAST

- Narrator
- Mother
- Andrew
- Father
- Grandma
- Grandpa

STAGING

Any space will do: a raised platform or the floor of the library, gymnasium, or classroom. This is an ideal play to perform as a second story when doing a presentation for other groups and parents and teachers because it can be played in whatever space the previous presentation happened. It does not make the technical demands of larger cast stories such as *The Fire Station*, *Jonathan Cleaned Up—Then He Heard a Sound*, or *Pigs,* and it may be done with minimal staging.

The NARRATOR is seated downstage right at the opening of the performance. GRANDMA and GRANDPA are seated on chairs and face upstage left, their backs to the audience.

MOTHER, FATHER, and ANDREW stand center stage. MOTHER and FATHER are wearing outdoor winter coats. MOTHER holds ANDREW's winter jacket and mittens.

SET DESIGN

There are six chairs on stage. The four at upstage right are used to make the car. The chairs on which the GRAND-PARENTS sit may be used later to create ANDREW's bed.

A set of steps (riser) is optional for walking upstairs/downstairs.

A screen, room divider, or rolling blackboard upstage left is useful for GRANDPA's and ANDREW's exits into the "bathroom."

PROPS AND COSTUMES

- ANDREW's favorite toy or blanket, which goes everywhere with him
- A cutout of a bush, sprinkled with snow, large enough to conceal ANDREW is positioned upstage right, or it may be held up by the NARRATOR for Andrew to hide behind.
- winter jackets, mufflers, hats, and gloves for the family
- ANDREW's snowsuit
- ANDREW's bed
- a blanket
- a pillow
- one or two pajama jackets
- a drawer or box upstage left and a clothes stand

NARRATOR:	This story is called *I Have to Go!* One day Andrew's mother and father were taking him to see his grandma and grandpa. Before they put him in the car his mother said:
MOTHER:	Andrew, do you have to go pee?
ANDREW:	No, no, no, no, no.
NARRATOR:	His father said very slowly and clearly:
FATHER:	Andrew, do you have to go pee?
ANDREW:	No, no, no, no, no.
NARRATOR:	Said Andrew.
ANDREW:	I have decided never to go pee again. *(FATHER and MOTHER set up the car by placing two chairs for the front seats and two chairs for the back seats, center stage.)*
NARRATOR:	So they put Andrew in the car, fastened his seat belt, and drove off.
ALL:	VAROOM.
NARRATOR:	They had been driving for just one minute when what do you think Andrew yelled? *(NARRATOR waits a beat to encourage participation.)*
ALL:	I HAVE TO GO PEE!

25

FATHER:	YIKES!
NARRATOR:	Said the father.
MOTHER:	OH NO!
NARRATOR:	Said the mother. Then the father said:
FATHER:	Now, Andrew, wait just five minutes. In five minutes we will come to a gas station, and then you can go pee.
NARRATOR:	Andrew said:
ANDREW:	I have to go pee RIGHT NOW!
NARRATOR:	So the mother stopped the car— SCREEEEECH. Andrew jumped out of the car and peed behind a bush. *(A freeze of a count of three to denote passing of time)*
NARRATOR:	When they got to Grandma's and Grandpa's house … *(GRANDMA and GRANDPA rise and come over to greet the family.)*
NARRATOR:	Andrew wanted to go out to play, but it was snowing and he needed his snowsuit. *(GRANDMA brings the snowsuit from the clothes stand.)*

NARRATOR:	Before they put on the snowsuit, the mother and father and the grandma and grandpa all said:
ALL:	ANDREW! DO YOU HAVE TO GO PEE?
NARRATOR:	And Andrew said …
ANDREW:	No, no, no, no, no.
NARRATOR:	So they put on Andrew's snowsuit. It had 5 zippers, 10 buckles, and 17 snaps. It took them half an hour to get the snowsuit on him. Andrew walked out into the backyard, threw one snowball, and what do you think he yelled?
ALL:	I HAVE TO GO PEE.
NARRATOR:	The father and mother and the grandpa and grandma all ran outside, got Andrew out of his snowsuit, and the father hurried him to the bathroom.
	(ANDREW and his FATHER run offstage, up left. The family gathers chairs, placing them as though around a dinner table facing in.)
NARRATOR:	When Andrew came back down they had a nice long dinner *(ANDREW yawns loudly)* and Grandma said:
GRANDMA:	I'll just go and make Andrew's bed. He must be tired.
NARRATOR:	And Andrew's mother went up to help her.

(Each carries a chair "upstairs." The others follow. A blanket, pillow, and pajamas are in a drawer by the clothes stand.)

NARRATOR: Before they put Andrew into bed, the mother and the father and the grandpa and grandma help change him into pajamas, then they ask:

(Stand around the bed masking ANDREW undressing)

ALL: ANDREW! DO YOU HAVE TO GO PEE?

NARRATOR: And Andrew said …

ALL: No, no, no, no, no.

NARRATOR: So the mother gave him a kiss, and the father gave him a kiss, and the grandma gave him a kiss, and the grandpa gave him a kiss, and they all stood and listened.

MOTHER: Just wait.

NARRATOR: Said the Mother:

MOTHER: He's going to yell and say,

FATHER/MOTHER: "I have to go pee."

NARRATOR: The father and the mother said at the same time.

FATHER: He does it every night. It's driving us crazy.

NARRATOR: The grandmother said:

GRANDMOTHER: I NEVER had these problems with my children.

NARRATOR: They waited for 5 minutes, 10 minutes, 15 minutes, **20 minutes**. The father said:

FATHER: I think he is asleep.

NARRATOR: The mother said:

MOTHER: Yes, I think he is asleep.

NARRATOR: The grandmother said:

GRANDMOTHER: He is definitely asleep and he didn't yell and say he had to go pee.

NARRATOR: Then Andrew said:

ANDREW: I wet my bed.

NARRATOR: So the mother and the father and the grandma and the grandpa all changed Andrew's bed and Andrew's pajamas. Then the mother gave him a kiss, and the father gave him a kiss, and the grandma gave him a kiss, and the grandpa gave him a kiss, and the grown-ups all went downstairs. They waited for:

MOTHER: 5 minutes.

FATHER: 10 minutes.

GRANDMA:	15 minutes.
GRANDPA:	20 minutes.
NARRATOR:	And from upstairs Andrew yelled:
ANDREW:	GRANDPA, DO YOU HAVE TO GO PEE?
NARRATOR:	And Grandpa said:
GRANDPA:	Why yes, I think I do.
NARRATOR:	Andrew said:
ANDREW:	Well, so do I.
NARRATOR:	So they both went to the bathroom and peed in the toilet.

(Grandpa and Andrew exit offstage and are no longer in sight of the audience. If no masking is available, they turn upstage and freeze.)

NARRATOR:	And Andrew did not wet his bed again that night—not even once.

(CAST moves to center stage and bows.)

Something Good

CAST

- Narrator 1/Julie
- Narrator 2/Andrew
- Tyya
- Father
- Friends 1 and 2 (may also play Store Lady and Female Customer)
- Store Lady
- Male Customer
- Female Customer
- Cashier (may also play Male Customer)

STAGING

A large space is required, such as a gymnasium. The audience is seated on both sides of two diagonal aisles that lead from the playing space to the last row of spectators. Masking tape is helpful for the CAST to create the aisles in the supermarket. Before the play begins and while the audience is being seated, both NARRATORS are onstage beside FATHER and TYYA. FATHER pushes the cart, looks at his shopping list, and scans the shelves (real or imaginary).

The NARRATORS sit side by side stage left or right, close to the audience. They share a bench or sit on stools, cubes, chairs, or a riser.

Exits and entrances are from off-stage, onstage, and from behind the audience.

SET DESIGN

- A low bench is required for the dolls, preferably leaning against a wall or backdrop.
- Bookshelves are ideal for display purposes. Paint easels may have posters attached to them, showing a variety of candies or fruits.
- A narrow table is required for the cash register and for counter space.

PROPS AND COSTUMES

The suggestions below are optional. The grocery store is such a familiar place that one or two displays or mime are sufficient to indicate the setting. The following ideas may appeal to students with an interest in arts and crafts. Also this might be an opportunity for an older group to work on the project with a younger group.

- three shopping carts (FATHER's cart already has some "good" grocery items in it.)
- FATHER holds a long shopping list
- shelves of goods: real (or cutouts of) cans, ice-cream cartons, or candy wrappers glued onto cardboard or paper. A display of oranges and one of apples stands at each end of the shelf, on which three or four life-sized cutout of dolls are displayed (it would be too taxing to use students, as they would have to remain motionless for a long time).
- a price tag that says $29.95
- a cash register (consider a toy)
- a reversible sign that says OPEN/CLOSED
- a wallet
- Costumes should give some indication of character and occupation; for example, the STORE LADY and the MALE CASHIER might wear aprons and/or nametags.

(The NARRATORS take their places, leaving TYYA and FATHER at center stage.)

NARRATOR 1: This story is called *Something Good*.

NARRATOR 2: It's the story about the day we went grocery shopping with our father and our younger sister, Tyya. I'm Andrew, and this is Julie.

NARRATOR 1: Tyya pushed the cart up the aisle and down the aisle.

(TYYA and FATHER wheel the cart up and down all the aisles.)

NARRATOR 2: Up the aisle and down the aisle.

NARRATOR 1: Up the aisle and down the aisle. Tyya said:

TYYA: Sometimes my father doesn't buy good food. He gets bread, eggs, milk, cheese, spinach—nothing any good! He doesn't buy ICE CREAM! COOKIES! CHOCOLATE BARS! Or GINGER ALE!

(By this time FATHER and TYYA have returned to the stage from the diagonal aisles through the audience.)

NARRATOR 2: So Tyya very quietly snuck away from Father and got a cart of her own.

(The cart is upstage of the NARRATORS.)

NARRATOR 1:	She pushed it over to the ice cream. Then she put 100 boxes of ice cream into the cart.
	(TYYA rapidly puts a pile of the cartons into the cart—100 are not required!)
NARRATOR 1:	Tyya pushed that cart up behind Father and said:
TYYA:	DADDY, LOOK!
NARRATOR 1:	Father turned around and yelled:
FATHER:	YIKES!
NARRATOR 1:	Tyya said:
TYYA:	DADDY! GOOD FOOD!
FATHER:	Oh, no.
NARRATOR 1:	Father said.
FATHER:	This is sugary junk. It will rot your teeth. It will lower your IQ. Put it ALL BACK!
NARRATOR 1:	So Tyya put back the 100 boxes of ice cream. She meant to go right back to our father, but on the way she had to pass the candy. She put 300 chocolate bars into her cart. Tyya pushed that cart up behind our father and said:
TYYA:	DADDY, LOOK!

NARRATOR 1:	Father turned around and said:
FATHER:	YIKES!
NARRATOR 1:	Tyya said:
TYYA/NARRATORS:	DADDY! GOOD FOOD!
	(NARRATORS speak at the same time as TYYA, to encourage the audience to participate in the refrain.)
FATHER:	Oh no.
NARRATOR 1:	Said our Father.
FATHER:	This is sugary junk. Put it ALL BACK!
NARRATOR 1:	So Tyya put back all the chocolate bars, except …
	(TYYA attempts to conceal one bar, but her FATHER and the NARRATORS give her a stern look and she puts it back.)
NARRATOR 2:	Then Father said:
FATHER:	Okay, Tyya, I have had it. You stand here and DON'T MOVE.
NARRATOR 2:	Tyya knew she was in BIG trouble, so she stood there and DIDN'T MOVE. Some friends came by and said:
FRIEND 1:	Hello, Tyya.

FRIEND 2:	Want to help us choose some candy?
NARRATOR 2:	Tyya didn't move.
	(*MALE CUSTOMER enters from the front row of the audience and grabs a cart. He does not look where he is going and wheels it over TYYA'S foot.*)
NARRATOR 2:	Still, Tyya didn't move.
	(*STORE LADY enters from offstage or from an aisle where she has been stocking shelves.*)
NARRATOR 2:	A lady who worked at the store came by and looked at Tyya. She looked her over from the top down, and she looked her over from the bottom up. She knocked Tyya on the head—and Tyya still didn't move. The lady said:
STORE LADY:	This is the nicest doll I have ever seen. It almost looks real.
NARRATOR 2:	She put a price tag on Tyya's nose that said $29.95, then she picked Tyya up and put her on the shelf with all the other dolls.
NARRATOR 1:	A man came along and looked at Tyya. He said:
MALE CUSTOMER:	This is the nicest doll I have ever seen. I am going to get that doll for my son.

NARRATOR 1:	He picked Tyya up by the hair. Tyya yelled very loudly:
TYYA:	STOP!
NARRATOR 1:	The man screamed:
MALE CUSTOMER:	EAAAAH! IT'S ALIVE!
NARRATOR 1:	And he ran down the aisle, knocking over a pile of 500 apples.
	(After he has knocked over the display, the MALE CUSTOMER exits upstage. Meanwhile the FEMALE CUSTOMER has entered the store from the nearest diagonal aisle and picked up the MALE CUSTOMER's cart.)
NARRATOR 2:	A lady came along and looked at Tyya. She said:
FEMALE CUSTOMER:	This is the nicest doll I have ever seen. I think I will buy this doll for my daughter.
NARRATOR 2:	She picked up Tyya by the ear. Tyya yelled as loudly as she could:
TYYA:	STOP!
NARRATOR 2:	The lady screamed:
FEMALE CUSTOMER:	EYAAAAH! IT'S ALIVE!
NARRATOR 2:	And she ran down the aisle, knocking over a pile of 500 oranges *(exits, rushing down the aisle)*.

NARRATOR 2:	Then Tyya's father came along, looking for our sister. He said:
FATHER:	Tyya? Tyya? Tyya Tyya? Where are you? ... TYYA! What are you doing on that shelf?
NARRATOR 2:	Tyya said:
TYYA:	You told me not to move and people are trying to buy me. WAAAAAHHHHH!
FATHER:	Oh, come now.
NARRATOR 1:	Father said.
FATHER:	I won't let anybody buy you.
NARRATOR 1:	He gave Tyya a big kiss and a big hug. Then we went to pay for all the food. *(The CASHIER has set up his counter and cash register and turned the CLOSED SIGN to OPEN.)*
NARRATOR 1:	The man at the cash register looked at Tyya and said:
CASHIER:	Hey, mister, you can't take that kid out of the store. You have to pay for her. It says so right on her nose: $29.95.
NARRATOR 1:	Father said:
FATHER:	Wait, this is my own kid. I don't have to pay for my own kid.

NARRATOR 1:	The cashier said:
CASHIER:	If it has a price tag, you have to pay for it.
FATHER:	I won't pay.
NARRATOR 1:	Said our father.
CASHIER:	You've got to.
NARRATOR 1:	Said the man. Father said:
FATHER:	NNNNO!
NARRATOR 1:	The man said:
CASHIER:	YYYYES!
NARRATOR 1:	Father said:
FATHER:	NNNNO!
NARRATOR 1:	The man said:
CASHIER:	YYYYES!
NARRATORS:	We all yelled:
ALL:	NNNNO!
NARRATOR 2:	Then Tyya quietly said:
TYYA:	Daddy, don't you think I'm worth $29.95?

FATHER:	Ah … Um … I mean … Well, of course you're worth $29.95.
NARRATOR 2:	Father reached into his wallet, got out the money, paid the man, and took the price tag off Tyya's nose.
NARRATOR 1:	Tyya gave Father a big kiss—SMMMERCCHH—and a big hug—MMMMMMMMMM—and then she said:
TYYA:	Daddy, you finally bought something good after all.
NARRATOR 2:	Then Father picked up Tyya and gave her a big long hug—and didn't say anything at all.

(CAST joins hands and bows) |
| ALL: | THE END |

David's Father

CAST

- Narrator
- Julie
- Moving Man with Spoon (also Stagehand and Sound Effects)
- Moving Man with Fork (also Stagehand and Sound Effects)
- Moving Man with Knife (also Grandmother's Voice and Sound Effects)
- David
- Mother's Voice (also plays one of the Big Grade 8 Kids)
- David's Father
- Cars/Drivers (three to six)
- Storekeeper
- Six big Grade 8 Kids

This can be a large cast show or reduced by double casting. One of the MOVING MEN could play the role of the STOREKEEPER, and the CARS/DRIVERS double as the GRADE 8 KIDS. This play lends itself well to older and younger students working together.

STAGING

A horseshoe (U shape). At the start of the play, the NARRATOR sits downstage and JULIE sits facing upstage, wearing a knapsack.

SET DESIGN

Locations are: street, JULIE's bedroom, DAVID's house, the store. JULIE's bed may be two chairs or a cushion and a blanket upstage right or left.

A small table is preset offstage with JULIE's and DAVID's dinner or may be preset upstage and covered with a cloth until needed in the play.

Chairs, cubes, or a bench represent the STOREKEEPER's counter and are brought onstage when needed. Toy steering wheels, though not essential, are fun for each DRIVER to simulate driving cars.

A screen, a room divider, or a rolling blackboard upstage center is used for exits and entrances and to mask backstage. It also serves as a backdrop to suggest different locations. A drawing/painting on chart paper or a colorful poster can be dropped down as needed.

Locations may be changed by an actor bringing in a prop or set piece.

PROPS AND COSTUMES

- JULIE's knapsack
- oversized spoon, fork, and knife—consider large plastic cookware or plastic beach toys
- a baseball for DAVID (unless mimed)
- the dinner: normal size for DAVID and JULIE, set up on a small table covered with a cloth
- JULIE's bed
- DAVID's FATHER's table and his dinner may either be "imagined" by the ACTORS and audience or could be illustrated. A photo of the meal may be enlarged to poster size and dropped down over the divider.
- steering wheels for DRIVERS/CARS
- a couple of toy wheels or tires, to be held up by the NARRATOR
- STOREKEEPER's counter: a bench, chairs, or a riser
- large paper bags with ice cream containers, potato chips, and candy
- a huge bandage for JULIE's elbow
- DAVID's FATHER needs to wear heavy boots and oversized clothing to give a "giant" impression
- an oversized dinner napkin
- GRADE 8 KIDS wear jeans, skirts, or shorts and shirts layered over T-shirts and leggings or shirts so that they can throw off the top layers easily. Each KID can throw off just one garment when running away.
- STOREKEEPER might wear an overall, jacket, or cap.

NARRATOR:	This story is called *David's Father*.
	(JULIE rises and begins to skip around the stage.)
NARRATOR:	Julie was skipping home from school. A man came out of a large moving van *(men enter from offstage center)* carrying a spoon—only it was as big as a shovel. Another man came out carrying a fork— only it was as big as a pitchfork. A third man came out carrying a knife—only it was as big as a flagpole.
JULIE:	Yikes, I don't want to get to know these people at all.
NARRATOR:	Said Julie and she ran all the way home and hid under her bed until dinnertime.
	(JULIE hides in her room—preset upstage right or left.)
MOTHER'S VOICE:	Dinnertime!
	(JULIE exits with knapsack, then reenters from "school." DAVID enters a moment later, from offstage center, plays with base- ball, real or mimed.)
NARRATOR:	The next day Julie was skipping home from school again. A boy was standing where the moving van had been. He said:
DAVID:	Hi, my name's David. Would you like to come and play?

NARRATOR:	Julie looked at him very carefully. He seemed to be a regular sort of boy, so she stayed to play. *(They play.)* At five o'clock from far away down the street, someone called:
MOTHER'S VOICE:	Julie, come and eat.
JULIE:	That's my mother.
NARRATOR:	Said Julie. Then someone called:
DAVID'S FATHER:	DAVID!!!
DAVID:	That's my father.
NARRATOR:	Said David. Julie jumped up in the air, ran around in a circle three times, and ran home, locking herself in her room until it was time for breakfast the next morning. *(JULIE exits into her room, freezes, and resumes the action after a moment.)*
NARRATOR:	The next day Julie was skipping home and she saw David again. *(DAVID has reentered from offstage center.)*
NARRATOR:	He said:
DAVID:	Hi, Julie, do you want to come and play?
NARRATOR:	Julie looked at him very, very carefully. He seemed to be a regular boy.

JULIE:	I'll stay and play.
	(They play ball or hide-and-seek or tag.)
NARRATOR:	When it was almost five o'clock, David said:
DAVID:	Julie, please stay for dinner.
NARRATOR:	But Julie remembered the big knife, the big fork, and the big spoon.
	(The knife, fork, and spoon appear above the screen or are carried onstage for an instant by the STAGEHANDS.)
JULIE:	Well, I don't know, maybe it's a bad idea. I think maybe … No. Good-bye, good-bye, good-bye.
	(JULIE starts to leave.)
DAVID:	Well, we're having cheeseburgers, chocolate milkshakes, and a salad …
JULIE:	Oh? I love cheeseburgers. I'll stay, I'll stay.
NARRATOR:	So they went into the kitchen. There was a small table …
	(DAVID removes the cloth, displaying dinner.)
NARRATOR:	With cheeseburgers, milkshakes, and salads. On the other side of the room there was an enormous table. On it was a spoon as big as a shovel, a fork as big as a pitchfork, and a knife as big as a flagpole.

(*An illustration or poster is hung over the back cloth that displays the food on the enormous table, or it may be left to the imagination of the audience as JULIE stands on tiptoe and stares up at it.*)

JULIE: (*Whispers*) David, who sits there?

DAVID: Oh, that's where my father sits. You can hear him coming now.

SOUND EFFECTS: **BROUM, BROUM, BROUM.**

(*Sound made by boots offstage. When DAVID's FATHER enters, he brings in his own chair and oversized cutlery.*)

NARRATOR: He opened the door. David's father is a giant. On his table there were 26 snails, 3 fried octopuses, and 16 bricks covered with chocolate sauce (*FATHER sits and eats facing upstage*). David and Julie ate their cheeseburgers and David's father ate the snails. David and Julie drank their milkshakes and David's father ate the fried octopuses. David and Julie ate their salads and David's father ate his chocolate-covered bricks. David's father asked Julie:

DAVID'S FATHER: Would you like a snail?

NARRATOR: Julie said:

JULIE: No thanks.

NARRATOR: David's father asked Julie:

DAVID'S FATHER:	Would you like an octopus?
NARRATOR:	Julie said:
JULIE:	No thanks.
NARRATOR:	David's father asked Julie:
DAVID'S FATHER:	Would you like a DELICIOUS chocolate-covered brick?
NARRATOR:	Julie said ...
JULIE:	No thanks, but please may I have another milkshake?
NARRATOR:	So David's father made her another milk-shake. When they were done, Julie said, very softly so David's father couldn't hear:
JULIE:	David, you don't look very much like your father.
DAVID:	Well, I'm adopted.
JULIE:	Oh.
NARRATOR:	Said Julie.
JULIE:	Well, do you like your father?
DAVID:	HE'S GREAT. Come for a walk and see.
NARRATOR:	Said David. So they walked down the street. Julie and David skipped and David's father went:

SOUND EFFECTS:	**Broum, Broum, Broum.**
NARRATOR:	They came to a road and they couldn't get across.
	(CARS enter from both stage right and left.)
NARRATOR:	But the cars would not stop for David. The cars would not stop for Julie. David's father walked into the middle of the road, looked at the cars, and yelled:
DAVID'S FATHER:	**STOP!**
NARRATOR:	The cars all jumped up into the air, ran around in a circle three times, and went back up the street so fast *(CARS exit)* they forgot their tires.
	(NARRATOR holds up two toy tires.)
NARRATOR:	Julie and David crossed the street and went into a store.
	(STOREKEEPER enters with counter, sets up some goods to buy.)
STOREKEEPER:	I don't like serving kids! *(FATHER waits by NARRATOR.)*
NARRATOR:	They waited 5 minutes, 10 minutes, 15 minutes—then David's father came in. He looked at the storekeeper and said:
DAVID'S FATHER:	THESE KIDS ARE MY FRIENDS!

NARRATOR:	The man jumped up into the air, ran around the store three times, and gave David and Julie 3 boxes of ice cream, 11 bags of potato chips, and 19 rolls of candy—FREE!
	(He puts the items into bags.)
NARRATOR:	Julie and David walked around the street and went around the bend. *(Enter BIG GRADE 8 KIDS.)*
NARRATOR:	There were 6 big kids from Grade 8 standing in the middle of the sidewalk. They looked at David. They looked at Julie and they looked at the bags of food. Then one big kid reached down and grabbed a box of ice cream. David's father came around the bend. He looked at the big kids and yelled:
DAVID'S FATHER:	Beat it!
NARRATOR:	They jumped out of their shirts. They jumped right out of their pants.
	(Each kid sheds one garment and runs off-stage.)
NARRATOR:	And ran down the street in their underwear. Julie ran after them, but she slipped *(she falls)* and scraped her elbow. David's father picked her up and put a special giant bandage on her elbow.
	(DAVID's FATHER has lifted JULIE onto the NARRATOR's stool to fix the bandage.)

JULIE:	*(Whispers)* Thanks.
	(DAVID's FATHER exits.)
NARRATOR:	Julie said:
JULIE:	Well, David, you do have a very nice father after all, but he is still kind of scary.
DAVID:	You think HE is scary?
NARRATOR:	Said David.
DAVID:	Wait till you meet my grandmother.
GRANDMOTHER'S VOICE:	DAVID!
	(CAST stands and bows.)

Jonathan Cleaned Up— Then He Heard a Sound

CAST

- Narrator 1/Subway Boss's Voice
- Narrator 2/Announcer's Voice
- Jonathan's Mother
- Jonathan
- Subway Passengers/City Hall Workers
- Five Men Who Sleep on the Couch/first man plays Stagehand 1
- Police Officer Who Watches TV/Stagehand 3
- Conductor Who Watches TV
- Passenger Who Steals the Refrigerator/Stagehand 2
- Passenger/Lady at Front Desk
- Mayor
- Old Computer Man/Computer Voice

The cast may be 15 or more, depending on single or double casting.

STAGING

The play can be performed on a conventional stage, in a library, gymnasium, or classroom. At the start of the play, the NARRATORS are onstage, JONATHAN's MOTHER is at the front door, upstage right, ready to go shopping. JONATHAN stands center admiring the clean rug. To prevent tripping hazards, the rug needs to be secured in some way!

Other CAST members are offstage, waiting for their first entrance up left.

The audience is seated on both sides of a wide central aisle that is also used for exits and entrances and as a possible additional acting space.

SET DESIGN

The walls of JONATHAN's living room are, if possible, rolling white boards, placed in such a way that exits and entrances are at stage right, left, and center.

Seats for the NARRATORS: stools, cubes, or chairs are at downstage right and left, close to the audience.

The "sofa" is angled or may face front and consists of four or five chairs close together, each with a cushion. (The chairs are later used to suggest different locations.)

A short bench, offstage, for the COMPUTER MAN'S office.

A hat/clothes stand, onstage or offstage to facilitate quick changes of character.

PROPS AND COSTUMES

- The stove is offstage (it is referred to but not seen).
- The refrigerator is a double-sided cutout: the front shows the doors closed, the back shows empty shelves. It can be propped against a "wall" near the upstage right exit, beside a trash can.
- The television can be a blank screen hung from one of the walls or imaginary.
- Costume pieces and appropriate props for the SUBWAY PASSENGERS/CITY HALL WORKERS: caps, hats, scarves, big glasses, an umbrella, briefcases, a file folder, note pads, a shopping bag, newspapers, magazines. Actors need to be responsible for their personal props/costumes for each role.
- Garbage for the PASSENGERS to discard may be placed in three labeled boxes offstage for the three subway stops. ACTORS can bring their own CLEAN trash: cans of pop, gum wrappers, bags of chips and pretzels, paper coffee cups, bottles of water.
- erasable white board pens
- handprints and footprints, with pieces of tape attached to place on the boards. This should take very little time in performance, literally seconds!
- a peaked cap and whistle for the CONDUCTOR
- a hat for the POLICE OFFICER
- a gold chain of office for the MAYOR
- a cell phone, printout of names and offices, and pencil in hair for the LADY AT FRONT DESK
- a waistcoat and eye shade for the COMPUTER MAN and a spoon to eat jam with. The computer is painted silver. Inside, handgrips and flashlights to facilitate movement by STAGE-HANDS. If the computer is placed on a wheeled board, one person could manage to move it. The computer is big enough

for actors to be concealed behind it. The computer requires narrow openings for the lights to shine through the cardboard box as well as all kinds of arrows, buttons, or felt stuck on or painted.

- flashlights covered with colored paper for lighting effect
- books and papers and files on the desk (bench) in the computer office—carried in by STAGEHAND 3 and/or COMPUTER MAN
- three flash cards: one says CITY HALL, one says MAYOR'S OFFICE, and one says JAM STORE
- four cartons of "jam" and one or two jars. The cartons are upstage of NARRATOR 1, who also displays the JAM STORE flash card. The others are shown by NARRATOR 2.
- a shopping bag
- a can of noodles
- a cloth for JONATHAN to wipe the boards (the walls of his apartment)

NARRATOR 1: This story is called *Jonathan Cleaned Up— Then He Heard a Sound*. Jonathan's mother went to get a can of noodles. She said:

MOTHER: Jonathan, please don't make a mess!

NARRATOR 1: When she was gone, Jonathan stood in the middle of the apartment and looked at the nice clean rug and the nice clean walls and the very, very clean sofa and said:

JONATHAN: Well, there is certainly no mess here.

NARRATOR 1: Then he heard a sound. It was coming from behind the wall.

(CAST of PASSENGERS creates the sound of a subway train.)

NARRATOR 1: Jonathan put his ear against the wall and listened very carefully. The noise sounded like a train. *(Sound cue)* Just then a wall slid open and a subway train pulled up and stopped.

(PASSENGERS enter in file formation, dispersing after the announcement. PASSENGERS deposit their garbage before exiting out of the front door.)

NARRATOR 1: Someone yelled:

ANNOUNCER'S VOICE: LAST STOP! EVERYBODY OUT!

NARRATOR 1:	Then little people, big people, fat people and thin people, and all kinds of people came out of Jonathan's wall, ran around his apartment, and went out the front door. Jonathan stood in the middle of the living room and looked around. There was writing on the wall, gum on the rug, a man sleeping on the sofa, and ...

(JONATHAN opens the fridge door by reversing the cutout to show the empty shelves.)

NARRATOR 1:	ALL the food was gone from the refrigerator.
JONATHAN:	Well.
NARRATOR 1:	Said Jonathan.
JONATHAN:	This is certainly a mess!
NARRATOR 1:	Jonathan tried to drag the sleeping man out of the door, but he met his mother coming in.

(The MAN continues to sleep.)

NARRATOR 1:	She saw the writing on the wall, the gum on the rug, and the empty refrigerator. She yelled:
MOTHER:	Jonathan, what a mess!
NARRATOR 1:	Jonathan said:

JONATHAN:	The wall opened up and there was a subway train. Thousands of people came running through.
NARRATOR 1:	But his mother said:
MOTHER:	Oh, Jon, don't be silly. Clean it up.
NARRATOR 1:	She went out to get another can of noodles, and Jonathan cleaned up.
	(JONATHAN throws the garbage into the trash can.)
NARRATOR 1:	When he was all done, he heard a sound. It was coming from behind the wall. He put his ear up against the wall and listened very carefully. The noise sounded like a train. *(Sound cue)* Someone yelled:
ANNOUNCER'S VOICE:	LAST STOP! EVERYBODY OUT!
NARRATOR 1:	And all kinds of people came out of Jonathan's wall, ran around his apartment, and went out the front door.
	(Each time this pattern is repeated: CAST enters as a subway train, then becomes individual characters who trash the apartment.)
NARRATOR 1:	This time there were ice cream cones and chewing gum on the rug, writing and footprints on the wall, two men sleeping on the sofa, and a police officer watching TV. Besides that, the refrigerator was gone!

NARRATOR 1: Jonathan got angry and yelled:

JONATHAN: Everybody out.

NARARATOR 1: Just then his mother came in. She saw the ice cream cones and chewing gum on the rug, writing and footprints on the wall, two men sleeping on the sofa, a police officer watching TV, and a big empty space where the refrigerator had been. Jonathan's mother said:

MOTHER: What have you done?

NARRATOR 1: Then she heard a noise. It was coming from behind the wall. She put her ear right against the wall and listened very carefully. The noise sounded like a train. *(Sound cue)* Just then the wall slid open and a subway train pulled up. Someone yelled:

ANNOUNCER'S
VOICE: LAST STOP! EVERYBODY OUT!

NARRATOR 1: And all kinds of people stepped out of Jonathan's wall, ran around his apartment, and went out the front door. There were ice cream cones, chewing gum, and pretzel bags on the rug, writing and footprints and handprints on the wall, and five men sleeping on the sofa. Besides that, a police officer and a conductor were watching TV and the fridge and stove were gone. Jonathan went to the conductor and said:

JONATHAN: This is not a subway station. This is my house!

NARRATOR 1:	The conductor said:
CONDUCTOR:	If the subway stops here, then it's a subway station! You shouldn't build your house in a subway station. If you don't like it, go see City Hall.
NARRATOR 2:	So Jonathan went to City Hall.
	(JONATHAN exits out of the front door and walks all round the audience before entering up from the center aisle. The CAST as CITY HALL WORKERS enter on stage as soon as JONATHAN has exited. They reverse the white boards. Each worker rushes around, texting, talking, or listening on a cell phone, locking up a door, or closing a briefcase. Meanwhile, as they mill around the space they manage to pick up most of the garbage on the floor of JONATHAN'S apartment, making the change to the new location. JONATHAN times his entrance according to the following cues.)
CITY WORKER 1:	Can't stop, late for my meeting.
CITY WORKER 2:	I'm off for lunch.
NARRATOR 2:	When Jonathan got here …
	(NARRATOR 2 holds up the CITY HALL flash card.)
NARRATOR 2:	He asked the lady at the front desk:

(LADY AT THE FRONT DESK has set up her chair down center left.)

JONATHAN: Excuse me, please, but there is a subway train that stops in my living room. What shall I do?

LADY AT DESK: You'll have to go and see the subway boss.

(She points vaguely in the direction of NARRATOR 1.)

NARRATOR 1: *(As SUBWAY BOSS)* Nothing I can do. You'll have to go and see the mayor.

NARRATOR 2: So Jonathan went to see the mayor.

(LADY AT FRONT DESK places her chair for the MAYOR downstage center right. She exits up left. The MAYOR enters from upstage center. He wears his gold chain of office around his neck. NARRATOR 2 holds up the MAYOR'S OFFICE flash card.)

NARRATOR 2: The mayor said:

MAYOR: If the subway stops there, then it's a subway station! You shouldn't build your house in a subway station. Our computer says it's a subway station, and our computer is never wrong.

NARRATOR 2: Then he ran out for lunch.

(MAYOR exits down the center aisle and sits behind the audience.)

NARRATOR 2:	In fact, everyone ran out for lunch.
	(All CITY WORKERS, except those needed for the next scene, rush off for lunch down the center aisle and sit behind the audience. They have removed the chairs upstage right except for one, center stage, which will become the computer office.)
NARRATOR 2:	And Jonathan was all by himself at City Hall. Jonathan started to leave, but on his way out he heard a sound.
	(JONATHAN follows the workers down the center aisle.)
COMPUTER MAN *(offstage)*:	Ooooooooh, I'm hungry.
NARRATOR 2:	Jonathan listened very carefully.
	(JONATHAN walks up and down the aisle, listening and looking, before returning to the stage.)
NARRATOR 2:	He walked up and down the hall and found the room from where the sound was coming.
	(STAGEHANDS bring in the computer, big enough to conceal them, the COMPUTER MAN, bench, books, files, and papers.)
NARRATOR 2:	Jonathan went in and there was a big, enormous, shining, computer machine. The computer was going:

COMPUTER VOICE:	Wing, wing, kler-klung, clickety clang.
NARATOR 2:	And its lights were blinking off and on. The voice was coming from behind it.
	(STAGEHANDS exit, pushing aside the machine.)
NARRATOR 2:	Jonathan squeezed in back of the machine and saw a little old man sitting at a very messy desk. The man looked at Jonathan and said:
COMPUTER MAN:	Do you have any blackberry jam?
JONATHAN:	No.
NARRATOR 2:	Said Jonathan.
JONATHAN:	But I could get you some. Who are you?
COMPUTER MAN:	I'm the computer.
NARRATOR 2:	Said the man. Now Jonathan was no dummy. He said:
JONATHAN:	Computers are machines, and you are not a machine. They go wing, wing, kler-klung, clickety clang.
NARRATOR 2:	The man pointed at the big computer and said:
COMPUTER MAN:	Well, that goes wing, wing, kler-klung, clickety clang, but the darn thing never did work. I do everything for the whole city.

JONATHAN:	Oh.
NARRATOR 2:	Said Jonathan, suddenly getting an idea.
JONATHAN:	I will get you some blackberry jam if you'll do me a favor. A subway station is in my house at 980 Yonge Street. Please change it.
COMPUTER MAN:	Oh, certainly.
NARRATOR 2:	Said the old man.
COMPUTER MAN:	I remember doing that. I didn't know where else to put it.
NARRATOR 2:	Jonathan ran out and passed all the offices with nobody there.

(Exits offstage and around the audience and onstage again to where NARRATOR 1 holds up the JAM STORE flash card.) |
NARRATOR 2:	He ran down the stairs and all the way to the jam store. He got four cases of jam. *(NARRATOR 1 hands him the cases.)* It took him three hours to carry them all the way back to City Hall. There was still nobody there. He carried the jam back behind the computer and put it on the floor.
COMPUTER MAN:	Now.
NARRATOR 2:	Said the old man.
COMPUTER MAN:	Where am I going to put this subway station?

JONATHAN: I know.

NARRATOR 2:   Said Jonathan. And he whispered in the
                   old man's ear. Then he left. But the old
                   man yelled after him:

                   *(STAGEHANDS reverse the boards in
                   JONATHAN's house.)*

COMPUTER MAN: Don't tell anyone the computer is broken.
                   The mayor would be very upset. He paid
                   ten million dollars for it.

                   *(He digs his spoon into the jam and eats
                   greedily. MOTHER enters from stage right
                   and stands on her living room rug.
                   JONATHAN exits up left and returns
                   through his own front door. The COMPUTER
                   MAN freezes, spoon in hand.)*

NARRATOR 2:   When Jonathan got home, his mother was
                   still standing on the rug because she was
                   stuck to the gum. Jonathan started wash-
                   ing the writing off the wall. He said:

JONATHAN: There will be no more subways here.

NARRATORS: And he was right.

                   *(CAST moves downstage, center, and trans-
                   forms into SUBWAY PASSENGERS. MAYOR
                   moves forward. Others freeze.)*

MAYOR: OH NO, not in my office!

                   (MAYOR steps back into line. All bow.)

Show and Tell

CAST

- Narrator
- Benjamin
- Baby Sharon's Voice
- Class of Students (any number)
- Teacher
- Principal
- Doctor
- Benjamin's Mother

STAGING

The story takes place in a kindergarten and works well as theater in the round. There are four gangways or aisles, referred to, going in a clockwise direction, as A, B, C, and D. BENJAMIN and his family are at A, STUDENTS and TEACHER entrance is at B, the PRINCIPAL enters at C, and the DOCTOR enters at D. The audience sits all around the playing space, marked out with masking tape, between each of the four aisles, also marked out. Chairs and benches are placed for adult audiences.

At the start of the play only the NARRATOR is onstage. BENJAMIN and his MOTHER are at the back of Aisle A, behind the rolling blackboard, which hides them from the audience. The CLASS OF STUDENTS is behind Aisle B, masked in the same way. With them is the actor who plays BABY SHARON's VOICE. The TEACHER and the PRINCIPAL are behind Aisle C and the DOCTOR is behind Aisle D, also behind a rolling board or room divider. Actors wait motionless until their entrance.

SET DESIGN

Two stools—one set between Aisles A and D, and one between Aisles B and C—for the NARRATOR, who moves between them and around the circle as needed. He stands center stage to introduce the story.

A small table and chair are placed just off center.

The rolling boards are decorated on both sides with children's artwork.

A baby basket with a baby doll inside is placed at Aisle A in front of the rolling board and is visible to the audience.

PROPS AND COSTUMES

- a large baby doll inside a baby basket and a shawl
- a knapsack for BENJAMIN
- several items that BENJAMIN finally brings to school for show and tell. Some suggestions to consider are: a snake or animal puppet wound around his neck, a battered Bowler hat, a Dracula mask, a rat in a cage, an oversized tramp's boot, and so on. These objects may be stored in a covered box behind Aisle A until needed at the end of the play.
- a knapsack, which contains one item—preferably of ACTOR'S choice—for show and tell for each student
- three cell phones: for the NARRATOR, PRINCIPAL, and MOTHER
- the DOCTOR's bag, which contains: a flashlight, four needles of ever-increasing size, and a rubber hammer. Other items might be a thermometer, a measuring tape, bandages and a

pair of scissors, a jar of strange cream, a large bottle of pills,
a huge spoon and a bottle of medicine, a tongue depressor,
and a long rubber tube. Items should be oversized and some-
what outrageous-looking.

- Costumes are everyday clothes appropriate for the characters:
- MOTHER, TEACHER, and PRINCIPAL add glasses, a tie, or
  costume piece to differentiate them from the students
- DOCTOR wears a white coat and stethoscope

NARRATOR:	This story is called *Show and Tell*. Benjamin wanted to take something really neat to school for show and tell. What are some of the things that you remember bringing to class in kindergarten and Grade 1?
	(The NARRATOR walks around the circle, speaking directly to the audience. He repeats the answers. After two or three replies, or none, he sits and continues the story.)
NARRATOR:	So Benjamin decided to take his new baby sister, Sharon. He went upstairs to get her.
	(Benjamin enters from behind the rolling board, in Aisle A, and puts the baby doll in his knapsack)
NARRATOR:	He picked her up, put her into his knap-sack and walked off to school.
	(BENJAMIN exits and joins the other students and they all enter class from Aisle B. They sit around the performance space in twos, threes, or fours, asking each other what they have brought for show and tell. BENJAMIN sits next to the ACTOR who is BABY SHARON's VOICE. The TEACHER enters from Aisle C and takes her place at the table.)
NARRATOR:	But when Ben sat down, his baby sister finally woke up. She was not happy inside the knapsack and started to cry:

BABY SHARON:	WAAA, WAAA, WAAA, WAAA, WAAA.
NARRATOR:	The teacher looked at Benjamin and said:
TEACHER:	Benjamin, stop making that noise.
NARRATOR:	Ben said:
BENJAMIN:	That's not me. It's my baby sister, Sharon. She's in my knapsack. I brought her for show and tell.
TEACHER:	Yikes!
NARRATOR:	Said the teacher.
TEACHER:	You can't keep a baby in a knapsack!
NARRATOR:	She grabbed Ben's knapsack and opened it up. The baby looked at the teacher and said:
BABY SHARON:	WAAA, WAAA, WAAA, WAAA, WAAA.
TEACHER:	Don't worry, Ben, I know how to take care of babies.
NARRATOR:	She said and picked up his baby sister and rocked her back and forth. Unfortunately, the teacher was not the baby's mother and she did not rock quite right. The baby cried even louder:
BABY SHARON:	WAAA, WAAA, WAAA, WAAA, WAAA.

(Students react with whispers of advice. The PRINCIPAL appears from behind Aisle C and enters the classroom.)

NARRATOR: The principal came running in. He looked at the teacher and said:

PRINCIPAL: Stop making that noise!

NARRATOR: The teacher said:

TEACHER: It's not me. It's Sharon, Ben's new baby sister. He brought her for show and tell. She won't shut up!

NARRATOR: The principal said:

PRINCIPAL: Ah, don't worry. I know how to make kids be quiet, don't I, kids?

CLASS: Yes, sir. *(The PRINCIPAL grabs the baby from the TEACHER.)*

NARRATOR: The principal picked up the baby and yelled:

PRINCIPAL: HEY, YOU! BE QUIET!

NARRATOR: The baby did not like that at all. She screamed really loudly:

BABY SHARON: WAAA, WAAA, WAAA, WAAA, WAAA.

PRINCIPAL: What's the matter with this baby? It must be sick. I'll call the doctor.

(He returns the baby to the TEACHER and gets out his cell phone.)

PRINCIPAL: This is Principal Major of Fitzhenry Elementary School. We have a sick baby in the kindergarten class. *(YELLS)* Of course it is urgent!

NARRATOR: The doctor came at once with a big black bag.

(The DOCTOR enters from Aisle D and puts her bag on the table.)

NARRATOR: She looked in the baby's eyes and she looked in the baby's ears and she looked in the baby's mouth. She said:

DOCTOR: Ah! Don't worry. I know what to do. This baby needs a needle.

(She opens her bag and takes out different items and holds them up, puts them back in the bag after each "Naaaah.")

DOCTOR: Bandage, Naaaah! Pills, Naaaah! Tape measure, Naaaaah! Hammer?

ALL: NAAAAH!

NARRATOR: Then the doctor got out a short needle and said:

DOCTOR: Naaaah, TOO SMALL.

NARRATOR:	The doctor opened her bag, got out a longer needle, and said:
DOCTOR:	Naaaah, TOO SMALL.
NARRATOR:	The doctor opened her bag, got out a really long needle, and said:
DOCTOR:	Naaaah, TOO SMALL.
NARRATOR:	The doctor reached into her bag, got out an enormous needle, and said:
DOCTOR:	Ahhh, JUST RIGHT.
ALL:	NAAAAH!
NARRATOR:	And when the baby saw that enormous needle, she yelled as loudly as she could:
BABY SHARON:	WAAA, WAAA, WAAA, WAAA, WAAAA.
NARRATOR:	Ben said:
BENJAMIN:	What's the matter with this school? Nobody knows what to do with a baby. I've got to call my mother.
	(The NARRATOR hands BENJAMIN his cell phone.)
NARRATOR:	Go ahead, call her.
	(While he dials, MOTHER enters from behind Aisle A. She has her cell phone with her. She looks frantically in and under the

baby's crib, waving SHARON's shawl. She listens to BENJAMIN.)

BENJAMIN: HELP, HELP, HELP! You have to come to school right away.

NARRATOR: The mother said:

MOTHER: Ben, your little sister is lost! I can't come to school. I have to find her.

BENJAMIN: She's not lost. I took her to school in my knapsack.

(During this conversation the baby has been placed on the table. She is still crying but not loud enough to drown the words.)

MOTHER: Oh, no!

NARRATOR: Yelled the mother. She ran down the street and into the school where the baby was yelling as loudly as possible.

(She exits at Aisle A and enters from Aisle B. The PRINCIPAL, the TEACHER, the DOCTOR, and the STUDENTS stand around BABY SHARON trying to calm her down.)

PRINCIPAL: BE QUIET!

BABY SHARON: WAAA, WAAA, WAAA, WAAA, WAAA.

DOCTOR: It won't hurt a bit.

BABY SHARON: WAAA, WAAA, WAAA, WAAA, WAAA.

(MOTHER enters and gets to SHARON.)

BABY SHARON: WAAA, WAAA, WAAA, WAAA, WAAA.

MOTHER: Mother's here, Sharon.

NARRATOR: Benjamin's mother picked up the baby and rocked her back and forth, back and forth, back and forth. The baby said,

BABY SHARON: Ahhhhhhhhh.

NARRATOR *(whispering)*: And went to sleep. The principal said:

PRINCIPAL: Oh, thank you! Oh, thank you! That baby was making so much noise it was making me feel sick!

DOCTOR: SICK? SICK?

NARRATOR: Said the doctor.

DOCTOR: Did that man say he was SICK? He must need a needle.

NARRATOR: So the doctor opened her bag, got out a short needle, and said:

DOCTOR: Naaaah, TOO SMALL.

NARRATOR: The doctor opened her bag, got out a longer needle, and you know what she said:

ALL: Naaaah, TOO SMALL.

NARRATOR:	The doctor got out a really long needle and said:
ALL:	Naaah, TOO SMALL.
NARRATOR:	The doctor reached into her bag, got out an enormous needle, and what did she say?
ALL:	Ahhh, JUST RIGHT.
NARRATOR:	The principal looked at that enormous needle and said:
PRINCIPAL:	WAAA, WAAA, WAAA, WAAA, WAAA.
NARRATOR:	And ran out the door.
	(The PRINCIPAL exits, continuing his screams, until he is behind Aisle C. The DOCTOR runs after him, calling:)
DOCTOR:	Wait, it won't hurt a bit!
MOTHER:	Now.
NARRATOR:	Said the mother.
MOTHER:	It's time to take this baby home.
BENJAMIN:	Right.
NARRATOR:	Said Ben.
BENJAMIN:	You can use my knapsack.
MOTHER:	What a good idea.

NARRATOR: Said his mother *(They exit.)*

DOCTOR *(offstage)*: Hold still.

TEACHER: Straighten up the room, children, and then you can get ready for show and tell.

(The STUDENTS and the TEACHER straighten the table. They sit in line and open their knapsacks ready for show and tell to begin.)

NARRATOR: Ben and his mother put the baby to bed. She went to sleep and didn't cry, not even once.

(BENJAMIN gathers up his things for show and tell.)

DOCTOR *(offstage)*: There now, that didn't hurt, did it?

(The PRINCIPAL enters from Aisle C, holding his arm, and runs once around the audience, chased by the DOCTOR.)

PRINCIPAL: WAAA, WAAA, WAAA, WAAA, WAAA.

(STUDENTS react to the noise but cannot "see" what's going on. The TEACHER claps her hands for silence.)

DOCTOR: Just one more jab …

(They both exit back to the "office" behind Aisle C. Meanwhile, BENJAMIN has had time to put on his hat, wind the snake

*around his neck, and is on his way to
school. MOTHER remains by SHARON.
BENJAMIN enters at Aisle B.)*

NARRATOR: Ben went back to school carrying some
                   strange things for show and tell.

                   *(The TEACHER claps her hands, and the
                   STUDENTS stand and hold up the things
                   they have brought. BENJAMIN joins them.)*

NARRATOR: And he wasn't out of place at all.

                   *(Freeze until the CAST is joined by MOTHER,
                   who holds the baby wrapped in a shawl, by
                   the TEACHER, NARRATOR, the PRINCIPAL,
                   and the DOCTOR. They walk around the
                   circle and bow four times to each section
                   of the audience.)*

From Far Away

CAST

- Saoussan Askar
- Reading Buddy
- Sister
- Mother
- Father
- Teacher
- Cast/Children of Beirut/Canadian Students (any number between 6 and 12)
- Sound Effects/Voice of Airplane Steward/Stagehands

STAGING

At the start of the play, SAOUSSAN and her READING BUDDY each sit on a riser or bench, downstage right and left. SOUND EFFECTS are upstage left.

The entire CAST is onstage, except for MOTHER, FATHER, and TEACHER, who are offstage. SISTER is seated on the cushion upstage of SAOUSSAN. The CAST is seated in a semicircle. READING BUDDY holds the letter SAOUSSAN has written to him/her (and is in the process of writing).

Exits and entrances are from offstage and onstage. ACTORS may step into a new role from their places in the circle.

SET DESIGN

A screen, room divider, or a rolling blackboard is upstage. A brightly colored cloth is draped from the board in SAOUSSAN's

home. When the play moves from Lebanon to Canada, the board is reversed to show a large map of the world, artwork, and/or charts typical of an elementary school classroom.

There is a small table and a chair, center stage.

PROPS AND COSTUMES

- two copies of SAOUSSAN's letter
- a pencil
- a drum, saucepan, and pieces of wood, saucepan lids, or a noise-maker to suggest the war and the sound of the roof falling down
- an envelope containing airline tickets
- a large, paper Halloween skeleton that can be taped up
- Halloween masks for every STUDENT
- a hijab: the traditional head scarf worn by MOTHER
- a flash card that says GIRLS
- a long dress or skirt worn by MOTHER
- two Halloween goodie bags containing treats
- The TEACHER might add a purse, scarf, or jacket for the meeting in the mall.
- a basket containing costume pieces/hats for STUDENTS to wear at the school Halloween party

When SAOUSSAN and her family move to Canada, SAOUSSAN's letter and pencil stay on the riser. At the conclusion of the story, in Canada, SAOUSSAN returns to the riser and finishes the letter to her READING BUDDY.

(As SAOUSSAN writes, she reads aloud.)

SAOUSSAN: Dear Reading Buddy, My teacher suggested that I write to you. I will tell you about myself. My name is Saoussan. I am seven years old and I am in Grade 2 now. I come from far away.

BUDDY: *(Reading aloud)* The place we used to live was very nice:

(CAST and SAOUSSSAN and her SISTER walk around the stage, greeting one another. Some boys begin a game, or chase each other; the girls stop and chat in groups.)

BUDDY: But then a war started.

(SOUND EFFECTS: One loud drumbeat and the CAST freezes the action for a moment before scattering in panic. SOUND EFFECTS continue, a boy falls, holding his arm, another helps him back to his place. The SISTERS run home; others scream and push their way back to their places and sit. BUDDY continues reading.)

BUDDY: Even where my sister and I slept there were holes in the wall.

(The girls lie down to sleep.)

Finally, one day there was a big boom.

	(A crashing sound. Her SISTER runs to the "wall," followed by SAOUSSAN. They crouch against it and manage to pull down the cloth.)
BUDDY:	And part of our roof fell in.
	(MOTHER AND FATHER enter from upstage.)
PARENTS:	We have to leave.
MOTHER:	There is no food.
FATHER:	And we are getting shot at.
SAOUSSAN:	My father left.
	(The FAMILY hugs good-bye. SISTER follows FATHER upstage, he exits. SISTER stands and waves, remains looking upstage.)
SAOUSSAN:	My father left and was gone for a long time. But one day …
	(SISTER hurries home, waving an envelope, and gives it to MOTHER.)
SISTER:	Mother, a letter came.
	(MOTHER opens the envelope and takes out three tickets.)
MOTHER:	Father has sent us tickets to go to Canada.
SAOUSSAN:	I did not know anything about Canada, but the next day I was on a plane going there.

(MOTHER has picked up cloth and cushions and placed them out of the way. The CAST moves across the stage and sits in the shape of an airplane. SOUSSAN sits huddled on the riser, her back to the audience.)

STEWARD: Fasten your seat belts, please.

BUDDY: As soon as the plane moved, I got sick. I stayed sick for the whole trip, which was two days long. I didn't like it. Nobody wanted to sit near me. Once we got to Canada …

(SAOUSSAN turns around, the family is reunited, and the CAST of passengers return to their places. STAGEHAND reverses the board showing Canadian motifs. He tapes the skeleton, backstage for later, and will hold up the flash card GIRLS as needed. MOTHER and SISTER exit offstage. Father stays with SAOUSSAN, holding her hand.)

SAOUSSAN: My father took me to a school and left me there, after he showed me the girls' bathroom.

(STAGEHAND holds up sign and remains upstage. The TEACHER enters and the STUDENTS group around her.)

SAOUSSAN: My father said:

FATHER: Be good and listen to your teacher.

SAOUSSAN: So I was good and I listened to my teacher.

(SAOUSSAN sits center, cross-legged, and gazes at the TEACHER. BUDDY holds his letter.)

TEACHER: Today, we are happy to welcome a new student, Saoussan Askar. She has come from far away, from Beirut in Lebanon.

(The TEACHER goes up to the world map and points to Beirut.)

TEACHER: I hope you will be happy here, Saoussan, and soon make lots of friends.

BUDDY: *(Reading)* I didn't know what she was saying because she did not know how to talk right. So I just sat and listened. Children were trying to talk to me.

STUDENT 1: Did you go to school in the place you come from?

STUDENT 2: Have you got any brothers and sisters?

STUDENT 3: Do you want to skip rope with us at recess?

BUDDY: I was not able to answer them because I didn't speak English.

SAOUSSAN: When I wanted to go to the washroom, I didn't know how to say, "I want to go to the washroom."

(SAOUSSAN crawls around the table and the students as BUDDY reads.)

BUDDY:	That's why I used to crawl to the door when the teacher turned her head and looked at the other side of the room. When someone opened the door, I crawled out and went to the washroom. I waited beside the door and crawled back in and went to my place.
SAOUSSAN:	Once, I crawled to the washroom …
	(STAGEHAND flips the board so that the skeleton is visible)
SAOUSSAN:	And saw a Halloween skeleton, only I did not know what Halloween was. I thought the skeleton was evil. I thought that people were going to start shooting each other here. *(SOUND EFFECTS, the CLASS and TEACHER are frozen until SAOUSSAN screams.)*
SAOUSSAN:	I screamed a very good scream: Aaaa ahh hhhh hhh hh!
BUDDY:	Everybody came running out of the rooms.
VOICES:	What's going on? Is someone hurt?
SAOUSSAN:	They thought someone was being killed in the bathroom. My teacher opened the washroom door.
	(TEACHER enters the washroom and removes the skeleton from the board. STAGEHAND flips the board around and TEACHER moves center with SAOUSSAN.)

SAOUSSAN:	She tried to tell me that it was Halloween time and the skeleton was made of paper.
BUDDY:	I didn't understand her and I didn't know what Halloween was. She jumped up and down and danced around to explain to me that Halloween is just fun.
	(STUDENTS join in, miming knocking on doors, calling:)
STUDENTS:	TRICK OR TREAT!
SAOUSSAN:	I thought the skeleton had made them all crazy and I screamed louder: Aaaa ahh hhhh hhh hh!
	(TEACHER motions STUDENTS to sit down. She puts her arms round SAOUSSAN, then sits on the chair.)
SAOUSSAN:	She hugged me to make me feel better. I felt as if my mother was hugging me. I jumped on her lap and pee went down my knees because I was scared to death. That happened so fast, and I felt guilty and ashamed of myself and I didn't know how to say, "I am sorry."
BUDDY:	But the big tear that went out of my eye said it for me. Someone phoned my father to come. Then I went and sat by the front door of the school till my father came and got me.
	(FATHER enters.)

SAOUSSAN:	This whole school is crazy and I don't want to stay here.
FATHER:	People in Canada are not going to start shooting each other. They dress up in funny clothes and wear masks and have fun at Halloween, you wait and see.
SAOUSSAN:	I had bad dreams about skeletons for a long time after that.
	(SAOUSSAN curls up in sleep. CLASS performs a skeleton dance, which begins and ends with a drumbeat cue.)
SAOUSSAN:	But finally I began to talk little by little. I learned enough English to make friends, and school started to be fun.
BUDDY:	Now I am in Grade 2/3 and I am the best reader and speller in the class.
TEACHER:	Who can spell rhinoceros?
	(Several hands are raised.)
TEACHER:	Yes, Angela.
STUDENT 4:	R-h-i-n-o-c-o-r-o-u-s.
TEACHER:	No. William?
STUDENT 5:	R-i-n-o-c-o-r-o-s. *(TEACHER shakes her head.)*
SAOUSSAN:	Me, please, teacher, I know.

TEACHER:	Saoussan.
SAOUSSAN:	R-h-i-n-o-c-e-r-o-s.
TEACHER:	Well done!
SAOUSSAN:	I read and write a lot of stories. I'm writing a story about coming to Canada. It begins like this: The streets were noisy with gunfire the day we …
TEACHER:	Saoussan, stop talking in class!
SAOUSSAN:	The teacher is now complaining that I never shut up. And this year when it was Halloween, I wore a mask and we had a party at school.
	(TEACHER brings out the basket of costumes, and students dress up. SISTER, also wearing a mask, enters with two goodie bags.)
SAOUSSAN:	Then I went with my sister trick-or-treating to the neighbors.
BUDDY:	We got candy and nobody shot at us the whole time.
	(STUDENTS, SAOUSSAN, and SISTER go into the audience saying, "Trick or treat." When BUDDY begins to speak again, STUDENTS and SISTER exit offstage or behind the audience. SAOUSSAN moves back to center stage and takes off her mask. MOTHER enters.)

BUDDY:	I decided that Canada is a nice place.
SAOUSSAN:	I changed my name from Saoussan to Susan. Do you like it, Mother?
MOTHER:	Susan is a nice name but not as nice as your own name, so change it back, please.
BUDDY:	The kindergarten teacher moved from our school.
	(TEACHER enters and greets the ASKAR family.)
SAOUSSAN:	But sometimes when I see her in the mall, I run to her and hug her and wish she was still my teacher.
	(SAOUSSAN returns to her riser and concludes her letter. PARENTS and TEACHER freeze.)
SAOUSSAN:	She was my first teacher in senior kindergarten and she helped me a lot. But she still does not let me sit on her lap.
BUDDY/ SAOUSSAN:	Goodbye, Saoussan.
	(CAST moves downstage center and bows.)

Pigs

CAST

- Narrator 1/Gate/Windows/Doors
- Narrator 2/Gate/Windows/Doors
- Narrator 3/Gate/Windows/Doors
- Narrator 4/Gate/Windows/Doors
- Megan
- Father
- Pigs (any number that the pigpen can accommodate, about 8 to 10)
- Principal
- Teacher
- Baby Pig
- Pig Bus Driver

STAGING

At the start of the play the NARRATORS are seated on benches, cubes, or chairs that are placed horizontally along two sides of the pigpen.

FATHER sits on a chair at a small table upstage right. MEGAN stands facing him.

The CAST is seated upstage around the playing space.

Exits and entrances are created by ACTORS stepping into the performance area as characters from their places on the floor and returning there when finished.

PIGS put on their snouts/ears/tails when the NARRATORS announce the title.

SET DESIGN

Masking tape in the shape of a square at center stage indicates the boundaries of the pigpen.

Doors, windows, and gates are formed by the NARRATORS, who hold pieces of wood or bamboo doweling, about 2.5 centimeters (1 inch) thick and 1.2 meters (4 feet) tall. The two NARRATORS at the outside of the quartet hold their dowels upright, and the two center-placed NARRATORS cross their dowels, thus forming a gate. When not speaking or creating images, NARRATORS remain seated.

FATHER'S coffee mug and newspaper is on the table.

A small table and chair represent the PRINCIPAL's office downstage left.

A coffee mug and newspaper/magazine are on his/her table.

There are three aisles: Aisle B is at center stage right, parallel with the NARRATOR'S bench. Aisle C is downstage center, to the right of the PRINCIPAL'S office. Aisle A is at upstage center left.

PROPS AND COSTUMES

- Mugs and a newspaper are set on the FATHER's and the PRINCIPAL's tables.
- PIG snouts can be made from sections of toilet paper rolls, fastened with elastic.

- Optional: Felt ears and string tails, or PIGS can wear a variety of the above. PIGS are of many colors so T-shirts and sweat-pants or shorts may be in different shades.
- BABY PIG wears a blue or pink bow in addition to the above.
- dowels for the NARRATORS
- a ribbon that Megan ties around BABY PIG's wrist
- a peaked cap for the PIG BUS DRIVER

(All four NARRATORS rise from their seats and speak the title in unison. On the word PIGS, the cast of PIGS put on their snouts, which have been placed in front of them. Once ready, the PIGS enter the pigpen and lie down, crouch, or just stand still.)

NARRATORS: This story is called *PIGS*.

NARRATOR 1: Megan's father asked her to feed the pigs on her way to school. He said:

FATHER: Megan, please feed the pigs, but don't open the gate. Pigs are smarter than you think. DON'T OPEN THE GATE!

(NARRATORS 1, 2, 3, and 4 form the gate at the front of the pigpen, and NARRATOR 1 speaks from his place there.)

NARRRATOR 1: Megan said:

MEGAN: Right, I will not open the gate. Not me. No sir. No, no, no, no, no.

(MEGAN skips to the pigpen. FATHER stays at the table, reading.)

NARRATOR 1: So Megan went to the pigpen. She looked at the pigs. The pigs looked at Megan. Megan said:

MEGAN: These are the dumbest-looking animals I have ever seen. They stand there like lumps on a bump. They wouldn't do anything if I did open the gate.

NARRATOR 1:	So Megan opened the gate just a little bit. *(MEGAN pushes the crossed dowels a little way apart.)* The pigs stood there and looked at Megan. They didn't do anything. Megan said:
MEGAN:	These are the dumbest-looking animals I have ever seen. They stand there like lumps on a bump. They wouldn't even go out the door if the house was on fire.
NARRATOR I:	So Megan opened the door a little bit more. *(See above.)* The pigs stood there and looked at Megan. They didn't do anything.
NARRATOR 2:	Then Megan yelled:
MEGAN:	HEY, YOU DUMB PIGS!
NARRATOR 2:	The pigs jumped up, knocked Megan down, and ran right over her—WAP-WAP-WAP-WAP-WAP—and out the gate. *(They run together round the stage and end up in the farmhouse kitchen. NARRATORS return to their places on the bench, except for NARRATOR 2, who continues to speak in place until NARRATOR 3 takes over.)*
NARRATOR 2:	When Megan got up she couldn't see the pigs anywhere. She said:
MEGAN:	Uh-oh, I am in big trouble. Maybe pigs are not so dumb after all.

NARRATOR 2:	Then she went to tell her father the bad news. When she got to the house, Megan heard a noise coming from the kitchen. It went:
PIGS:	OINK, OINK, OINK.
MEGAN:	That doesn't sound like my mother. That doesn't sound like my father. That sounds like pigs.
NARRATOR 2:	She looked in the window.
	(NARRATORS create a three-sided window by holding up their sticks.)
NARRATOR 2:	There was her father, sitting at the breakfast table. A pig was drinking his coffee. A pig was eating his newspaper. And a pig was peeing on his shoe.
FATHER:	Megan!
NARRATOR 2:	Yelled her father.
FATHER:	You opened the gate. Get these pigs out of here.
NARRATOR 3:	Megan opened the front door a little bit.
	(NARRATORS 1, 2, and 4 transform the window into the front door.)
NARRATOR 3:	The pigs stood and looked at Megan. Finally Megan opened the front door all the way and yelled:

(NARRATORS, except for NARRATOR 3, return to their bench.)

MEGAN: HEY, YOU DUMB PIGS!

NARRATOR 3: The pigs jumped up and ran right over Megan—WAP-WAP-WAP-WAP-WAP—and out the door. Megan ran outside. She chased all the pigs into the pigpen and shut the gate.

(NARRATORS repeat the gate procedure as previously.)

NARRATOR 3: Then she looked at the pigs and said:

MEGAN: You are still dumb, like lumps on a bump.

NARRATOR 3: Then she ran off to school.

(MEGAN exits at Aisle C. The PRINCIPAL enters from his place on stage through Aisle B and sits in his office. The PIGS run there across the stage.)

NARRATOR 3: Just as Megan was about to open the front door, she heard a sound:

PIGS: OINK, OINK, OINK.

MEGAN: That doesn't sound like my teacher. That doesn't sound like my principal. That sounds like pigs.

(NARRATORS 1, 2, and 4 create three sides of the window frame.)

NARRATOR 3:	Megan looked in the principal's window. *(PIGS respond according to NARRATOR 3's description.)* There was a pig drinking the principal's coffee. A pig was eating the principal's newspaper. And a pig was peeing on the principal's shoe. The principal yelled:
PRINCIPAL:	Megan, get these pigs out of here!
	(MEGAN runs around and enters at Aisle B. NARRATORS 1–4 create the front door. PIGS freeze.)
NARRATOR 4:	Megan opened the front door of the school a little bit. The pigs didn't do anything. She opened the front door a little bit more. The pigs still didn't do anything. She opened the door all the way and YOU know what she yelled:
	(NARRATORS join in the familiar phrases to encourage the audience to participate.)
ALL:	HEY, YOU DUMB PIGS!
NARRATOR 4:	The pigs jumped up and ran right over Megan and out the door.
PIGS:	WAP- WAP-WAP-WAP-WAP.
	(The PIGS run out and return to their original places, upstage, and freeze.)
NARRATOR 4:	Megan went into the school.

(The TEACHER enters.)

MEGAN: That's that! I finally got rid of all the pigs. Then she heard a noise:

(BABY PIG waddles up behind her.)

BABY PIG: OINK, OINK, OINK.

NARRATOR 4: Megan turned around and there was a new baby pig. The teacher yelled:

TEACHER: Megan, get that dumb pig out of here!

NARRATOR 4: Megan said:

MEGAN: Dumb? Whoever said pigs were dumb? Pigs are smart. I am going to keep it for a pet.

(MEGAN takes a ribbon out of her pocket and ties it around BABY PIG's wrist. She walks with BABY PIG to Aisle B.)

NARRATOR 4: At the end of the day they waited for the school bus. It finally came.

(The NARRATORS place the benches or cubes in the shape of a bus and raise their sticks to become the doors. PIGS get inside the bus, and one PIG wears a peaked cap as the BUS DRIVER.)

NARRATOR 1: As Megan walked up to the door, she heard someone say:

PIG DRIVER:	OINK, OINK, OINK.
NARRATOR 1:	Megan said:
MEGAN:	That doesn't sound like the bus driver. That sounds like a pig!
BABY PIG:	OINK, OINK, OINK.
NARRATOR 1:	She climbed up the stairs and looked in the bus. There was a pig driving the bus, pigs chewing the seats, and pigs lying in the aisle.
NARRATOR 2:	The doors shut and the bus started down the road. It drove all the way to Megan's farm, through the barnyard, and right into the pigpen. The pigs got out, the gates shut.

(NARRATOR/GATES do so.) |
NARRATOR 3:	Megan got out of the bus, walked across the barnyard, and marched into the kitchen. She said:
MEGAN:	The pigs are back in the pigpen. They came back by themselves. Pigs are smarter than you think.
NARRATOR 4:	And Megan never let out any more animals.
MEGAN:	Well, maybe when I go to the zoo …
NARRATORS:	At least not any more pigs.

(PIGS remove snouts, etc., and transform into elephants and walk around the stage. CAST bows.)